KT-409-428

SCHOOL

Mr Field

Chemistry teacher
Age: 48 years
Special features: lab coat
Weak point:
prone to fainting
Favourite phrase:
'Do you smell gas?'

SAINT BARNABAS

SCHOOL

Mrs Moray

History teacher
Age: 45 years
Special features:
prim appearance
Weak point: frustration
with Mr James
Favourite phrase:
'Let's all keep calm.'

Mrs MacNee

Maths teacher
Age: 53 years
Special features: cardigan
Weak point: hates fuss
Favourite phrase: 'Tea and biscuits, anyone?'

Mr James

Headmaster
Age: 59 years
Special features:
pinstripe suit
Weak point:
panics under pressure
Favourite phrase: 'Get out of my sight.'

MORTYMER Keene

Attack of the SLIME!

Tim Healey and Chris Mould

SAINT BARNABAS SCHOOL

Mortimer Keene

Pupil
Age: 8 years
Special features: specs
Weak point: none!
Favourite phrase:
'Hurrah for slime!'

SAINT BARNABAS SCHOOL

Mr Bevan

English teacher
Age: 24 years
Special features: bow tie
Weak point: laughs at
Shakespearean jokes
Favourite phrase:
'Well said, old mole.'

Mr Smart

Woodwork teacher
Age: 42 years
Special features:
sticking-out ears
Weak point: no sense
of humour
Favourite phrase: 'Are
you trying to be funny?'

Mr Green

Art teacher
Age: 38 years
Special features:
corduroy jacket
Weak point: easily bored
Favourite phrase: 'How
long till lunchtime?'

It struck without warning
And there was no time
To ward off the monstrous
Attack of the **slime**.

It moved down a corridor,
Covered the floor,
And silent as night
It oozed under a door.

It entered a maths class
Where Mrs MacNee
Was setting a problem
To kids from Year Three.

And then into English
Where young Mr Bevan
Was speaking of

Shakespeare

To some of Year Seven.

'Last week,' said the teacher,
'We talked about rhyme.
This week for a change
We'll be dealing with…

SLIME!'

SLIME IN THE DOORWAY!

Kids were aghast
And made for the playground
Incredibly fast.

But still it kept coming!

In almost no time

The foul-smelling gollops

Of **slime upon slime**

Had entered the kitchen
The hall and the gym;
The whole of reception
Was full to the **brim.**

Part Two

Up in the staff room,
With a low moan,
The anxious headmaster
Reached for the phone.

'Police? Thank goodness,
It's Mr James calling,
My school's full of slime
And the stench is appalling.'

'Slime!' he repeated,
'I tell you, it's true!
It looks something like jelly
And something like glue.'

Down in the Music Room

Emily Bruce

Tried to hold back the flow

But that was no use.

Oliver Morris
Was suddenly sick.
'Let's get to the playground,'
Cried Emily, 'quick!'

Out in the playground
Pupils assembled.
Some of them shivered
And some of them trembled

As the **slime** sealed its grip
On the whole lower floor.
It had taken their classrooms
And still wanted
more!

It was almost uncanny:
Wherever they ran
The slime seemed to follow
Like that was its plan!

Slime in the
cloakrooms,

Slime in
the loos,

Slime in their pockets

And **slime** in their shoes…

Slime in the satchels,

Slime in their hair,

Slime on their fingers,

Slime everywhere!

It was driving them crazy,
They'd all had enough.
Where had it come from
This horrible stuff?

Part
Three

Up in the science lab
Mortimer Keene
Sat tinkering with
His Slime-making Machine.

It really did work!
This thing was fantastic
Just cobbled together
From tins and elastic!

With chemicals mixed
In a large tube of glass
Borrowed from Mr Field's
Chemistry class.

No abracadabras,
No waving of wands,
Just a knowledge of pi
And **molecular bonds**.

'I'm Mortimer Keene!
I am the creator
Of a truly remarkable
Slime generator.

Let's keep this thing going,'
He thought with a grin,
Then scooped up and tipped
Some more chemicals in.

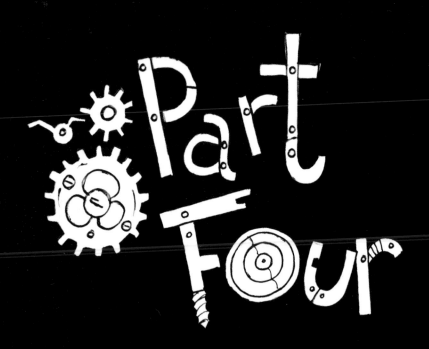

Part Four

Out on the sports field
Mrs MacNee
Was helping her maths class
Into a tree.

Kids from Year Seven
Were climbing a shed
On which Mr Bevan
Sat looking half dead.

While Mr Smart's woodwork class
Scurried about
Building a dam

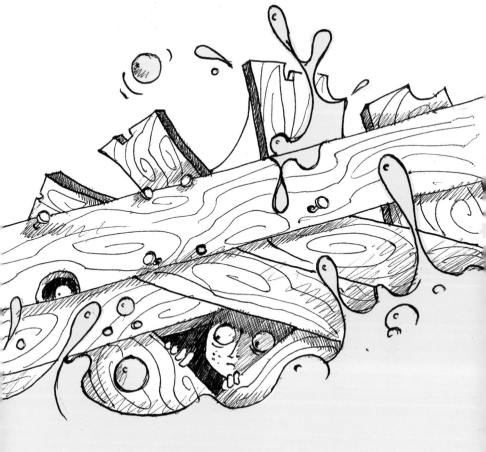

To keep the
slime out.

Up in the staff room
The headmaster had snapped.
'It's everywhere now!
We are trapped!
We are trapped!'

'Calm down Mr James,'
Said Mrs Moray.
'We could fashion a boat
Or a raft should I say,

And assemble at once
An emergency force
To ride on the **slime**
And discover its source!'

'BRAVO!'

cried the teachers
They cried it with zest

(Except poor Mr James
Who was still looking stressed).

A task force of three
Set off straight away:
Mr Singh, Mr Green
And bold Mrs Moray.

They used a large blackboard,
Crouched down on all fours,
And rowed out on the **slime**
Using textbooks for oars.

Out through the corridors,
Bobbing and weaving,
Tilting and wobbling,
Rolling and heaving,

Surfing each crest,
Descending each trench,
Jolted by rivers of
Gloop and of stench.

Over torrents of **slime**
Went the brave little crew,
To the science lab door
Where they struggled on through.

To find Mortimer Keene

At the scene of the crime!

Mortimer Keene

At the source of the slime!

'Turn that thing off!'
Cried Mrs Moray,
In a voice that was choked
With alarm and dismay.

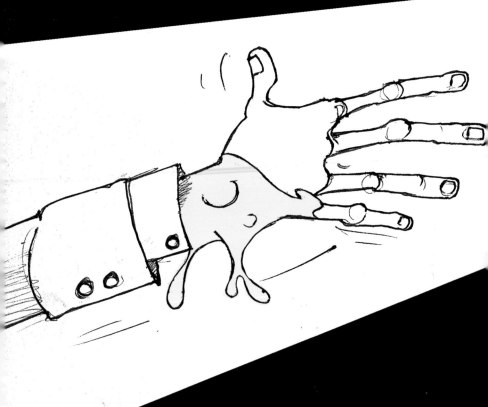

'Switch it off now!'
Mr Singh made a grab
For the switch that sent torrents
Of slime from the lab.

But Mortimer Keene
Held fast to the switch.
His eyes were ablaze,
He was starting to twitch

Like a madman possessed
By his own weird creation,
Obsessed with his mission
Of **slime generation.**

Mr Green grabbed his hand,
And he pulled it away.
'That's quite enough
Mortimer, lad, for one day.

There's nothing intrinsically
Wrong with your slime;
It's just in the wrong place
And at the wrong time.'

Mr Singh found the switch;
And he turned it to off.
The machine gave a **shudder**,
A clatter and cough.

Then one final rattle
And stopped with a
thud.
And that was the end of
The whole monstrous flood.

The nightmare was over
And Mortimer Keene
Was whisked off to hospital
Far from the scene.

The doctors declared
That the boy wasn't bad.
'Far too much homework
Has driven him mad.

An excess of homework
Is bad for the brain.
But with six months in bed
He'll be better again.'

Said Mrs Moray:
'We must close down the school
To clear up the mess;
It's a firm and fast rule.

You must all stay away
For a fortnight or more.
Only members of staff
May now pass through this door.'

'Close down the school…
…just as I feared, '
Mr James muttered glumly,
But the school kids all cheered.

'Close down the school!'
Loud came the call.
'We must all stay away!
Not so bad after all!

Two weeks off school
And its dreary routine!
Hurrah for the **slime…**

…and for
Mortimer Keene!'

Following these events,
Mr James retired as
headmaster of St Barnabas
School and Mrs Moray
became headmistress, a
post she still holds today.

Mortimer's **Slime** Plan!

Mortimer's **Slime** Machine!

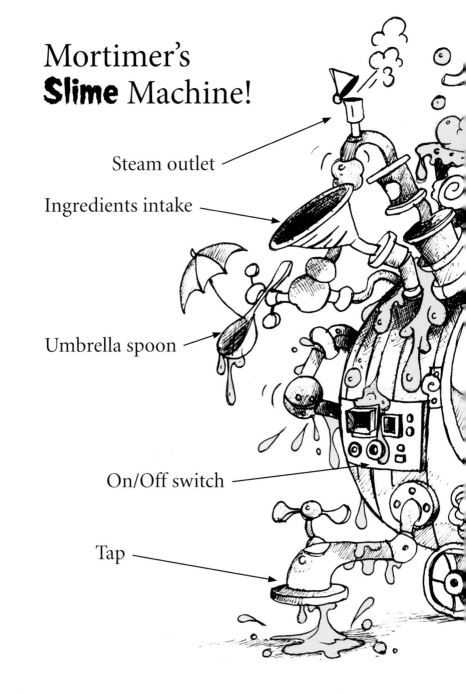

Steam outlet

Ingredients intake

Umbrella spoon

On/Off switch

Tap

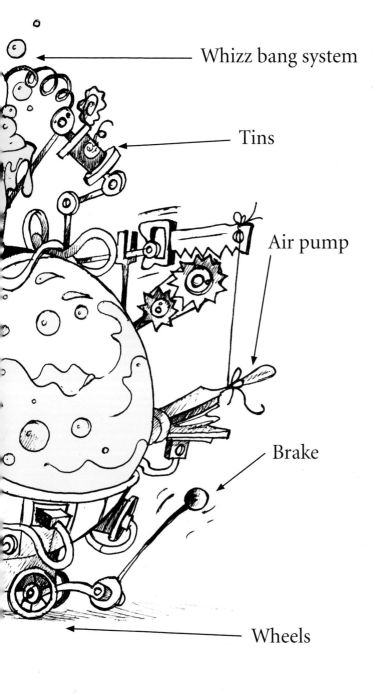

Whizz bang system

Tins

Air pump

Brake

Wheels

A-Z of Slime

Arctic slime – massive blobs of goo found floating in the Arctic sea.

Bitumen – inflammable slime!

Clammy – how cold slime feels to the touch.

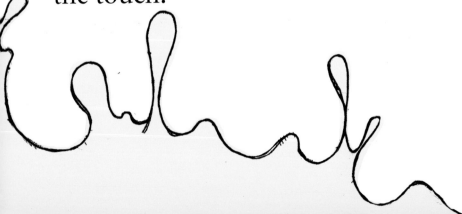

Digestive system – slime-producing cells throughout our bodies. Stay slimy inside!

Edible slime – slime that can safely be eaten, even the revolting bits of gloop in soft-boiled eggs.

Flubber – rubbery slime (from flying rubber).

Gloop, goo, gunge and gunk – popular terms for any thick, runny substance.

Hagfish – nature's champion slime-maker, also known as the 'slime eel'.

Indigo Slime – a German punk rock band of the 1980s.

Jelly – a favourite dessert for slime fans.

Keene, Mortimer –
a leading expert on slime and
slime manufacture.

Luminous slime – some
centipedes, squids and worms give
off a slime which glows in the dark!

Mucus – a slimy film given off
by many creatures.

Natural slime – slimes found in the natural world, such as algae, bitumen and mucus.

Ooze – to flow or leak out slowly, which is what slime generally does.

Protective slime – fish, snakes, slugs and snails all have a slimy mucus coating for protection against infection.

Quantum slime – science exploring the tiniest quantities of slime.

Red slime – one of the oldest life forms on earth, dating back at least 3.5 billion years.

Slime – any slippery, sticky, gooey material.

Toads – are not slimy! They actually have dry, warty skin. It's frogs that are slimy.

Uliginous – of a slimy or oozy nature.

Viscous – of a thick and sticky nature.

Wobble – what a mass of slime is prone to do when shaken.

X-rated slime – slime so disgusting that it is recommended for viewing by adults only.

Yuck – a common response to x-rated slime.

Zero slime tolerance – policy aiming to make public places totally slime-free.

Make your own Slime!

Follow these step-by-step instructions to make slime as yucky as Mortimer's!

What you need:

- Medium bowl
- 1 cup water
- 1 cup cornflour
- Green food colouring

Steps:

1. Pour 1 cup of cornflour and 1 cup of water into the bowl.

2. Mix the two together with your hands until it becomes gooey and doughy.

3. If it's not thick enough, add more cornflour or if it's too thick, just add more water.

4. Once the texture is thick and smooth, add green food colouring to achieve icky, green **gooey slime!**

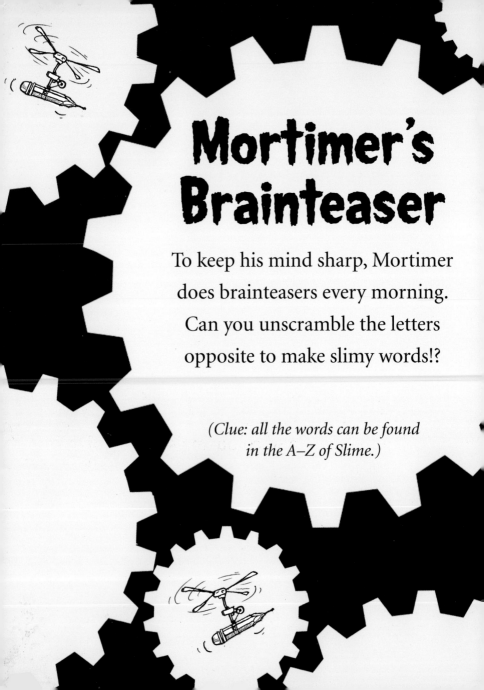

Mortimer's Brainteaser

To keep his mind sharp, Mortimer does brainteasers every morning. Can you unscramble the letters opposite to make slimy words!?

(Clue: all the words can be found in the A–Z of Slime.)

1. **elsim** 6. **rebbflu**

2. **blewob** 7. **umsuc**

3. **ezoo** 8. **soucsiv**

4. **lejly** 9. **knug**

5. **poogl** 10. **ogo**

Besides working on slime manufacture, Mortimer has been exploring many other ideas. He is working on:

1. A flying desk

2. Invisible books

3. Radio-controlled teachers

4. A cure for baldness

5. Rain-making satellites

6. A musical umbrella

7. Light-sensitive, self-opening curtains

8. Burgerbeams for beaming burgers to your plate

9. X-ray spectacles

10. Odourless feet